RABBIT & BEAR

A Bad King is a Sad Thing

STORY BY
JULIAN GOUGH

ILLUSTRATIONS BY
JIM FIELD

HODDER

First published in Great Britain in 2021
by Hodder Children's Books

This paperback edition published in 2022

A Catalogue record for this book is available
from the British Library

Hardback ISBN: 978 1 444 93746 6
Paperback ISBN: 978 1 444 93747 3

Printed and Bound in China by RRD Asia Printing Solutions Limited

MIX
Paper from
responsible sources
FSC® C104740

The paper and board used in this book are made from wood from responsible
sources.

Hodder Children's Books
A division of Hachette Children's Group
Carmelite House
50 Victoria Embankment
London EC4Y 0DZ

An Hachette UK Company
www.hachette.co.uk

THE RABBIT AND BEAR BOOKS:

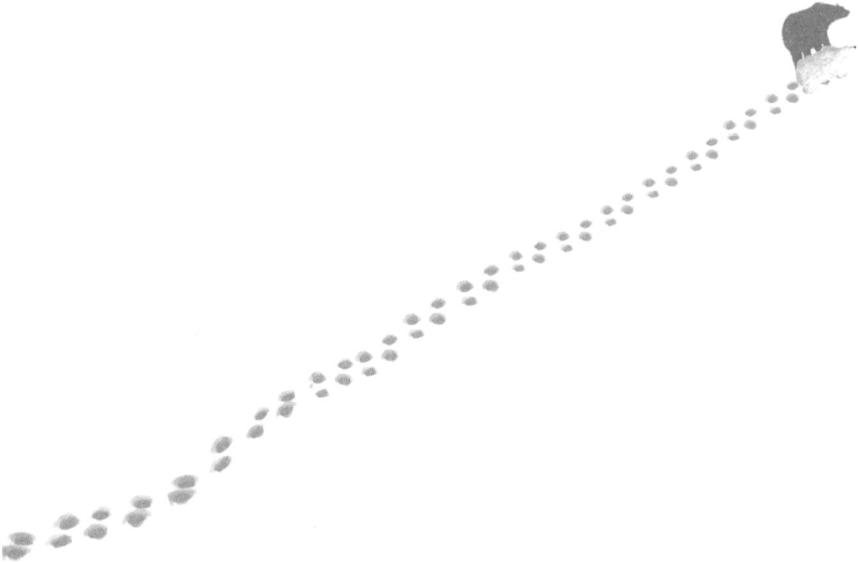

For Eliz Hüseyin, who gave me
my first break in the children's
picture book industry.
Thanks, Eliz!

J.F.

●

For my son Arlo, who arrived
as I was writing this book.
I love you.

J.G.

Rabbit was having a deep, peaceful winter sleep ... until he dreamt Wolf was about to eat him.

"AAAaaa*AAAaaa***AAAHHHHH!!!**"

Rabbit bounced awake. "Oh, what a *relief!* Only a dream." He yawned, and tried to stretch. "Wait, this isn't my lovely, big burrow. Why am I in a tiny, smelly cave?"

"Hrmmfff ... don't call me schmelly," said Wolf. His voice was a little muffled, because ...

"Oh no! I'M IN WOLF'S STINKY MOUTH!!!" shouted Rabbit.

As Wolf opened his mouth
to say, "It's NOT stinky!",
Rabbit leaped free.

"Come back, you cowardly breakfast!" cried Wolf, and chased Rabbit out of his burrow, down the hill, and up the other side.

Rabbit burst into Bear's cave, gasping, and shook Bear awake.

"Hmmmm …?" said Bear. "Oh! What is *Wolf* doing here, Rabbit?"

"HE'S—" But Wolf slapped a paw over Rabbit's mouth.

"… visiting you, dear Bear!" said Wolf. "For Company. Perhaps we could play a board game. Just you and me … and some of your more delicious friends …"

"Mmm! Nnnnnn! MMMMMM!" said Rabbit.

Bear frowned at Wolf. "But you always argue with me about the rules—"

"No I don't!" cried Wolf.

"—and you make sneaky, illegal moves—"

"Never!" cried Wolf, and ran out of the cave carrying Rabbit.

"—and!" said Bear, grabbing Wolf by the ear, "you eat my friends when I'm not looking."

"Ouch ... NO! Well, yes," said Wolf, as Rabbit wriggled free. "But I would probably only eat a couple of your *smallest* friends. You have so many, you won't even miss them."

"*I* will miss me!" said Rabbit, and hid behind Bear.

"You are not here to play board games, Wolf," said Bear. "Why are you here?"

Wolf sighed. "I'm totally *starving*." His belly rumbled in agreement. "This winter's gone on too long. There's nothing left to eat in the Dark Woods."

"Then STARVE!" shouted Rabbit. "Come on, Bear, make Wolf go away!"

8

"But ..." Bear wished she was awake enough to solve this difficult problem. "Perhaps we could share some of our food ..."

"NO!!! Get lost, Wolf!" From behind Bear's knee, Rabbit pointed at Wolf. "This is *our* Valley, not *yours*."

Wolf snarled, but he was too weak with hunger to fight. With a last, angry swish of his tail, he slunk off towards the Dark Woods.

"Hurray!" shouted Rabbit. "No more Wolf! Everything is perfect!" And Rabbit hugged Bear's tummy.

But Bear was distracted.

"Look ..." she said. "Something strange is coming towards us." They squinted as a large, dark shape strode swiftly across the frozen lake.

"It's like a bear!" Rabbit
said. "But bigger!"
"I have a bad feeling
about this," said Bear.

The dark shape came closer and closer, faster and faster, from the lake on to the beach, and then up the hill ...

Rabbit blinked into the glare of the low winter sun, trying to understand what he was seeing.

"Who ... or what ... are you?" he stammered.

"*Me?*" said the shape, in a deep voice. "I'm an icebear, of course."

But the voice seemed to come
from *beside* the huge shape. How odd …

Rabbit blinked again. Ah! He had been
staring at a shadow. The shadow cast
by a huge, white animal against the white
snow.

"Are there any … wolves around here?"
asked the Icebear.

"No," said Rabbit, proudly. He swung a
stick like a sword, but so wildly that he hit
himself on the back of the head. "Ouch …
We got rid of the last of THEM."

"Good," said the Icebear. "I don't like
wolves … What a perfect, uninhabited
valley!"

"What does uninhabited mean?" said
Bear.

"It means NOBODY lives here," said
the Icebear, and he walked straight
into Bear's cave without asking.

"But *we* live here!" said Bear, puzzled.

"And I'm SOMEBODY!" said Rabbit.

The Icebear stuck his head back out

of Bear's cave so fast, Rabbit fell over backwards.

"Really?" said the huge Icebear. "Hmmm. Can you hurt me? Kill me? Eat me?"

"Um … no," said Rabbit.

"Then you're not *somebody*. You're just food that no one has bothered to eat."

Rabbit spluttered in shock.

ROA

"But I won't eat you ... yet," said the Icebear. "I need slaves, to build a Palace. This cave is far too small for me!"

"Palace?" said Bear, even more puzzled.

"For the King," said the Icebear.

"But we don't *have* a king," said Rabbit.

"You will in a minute," said the Icebear. And he roared so loud that all of Rabbit and Bear's friends came running, jumping, and flying to see. Even Mole started tunnelling, but the frozen ground slowed him down.

"That's better," said the Icebear.
"*I claim this valley in the name of the King!* There, done."
"But ... who *is* the king?" squeaked Mouse.
"*I am*," said the Icebear. "And now all of you are my slaves. Go build me a Palace."

"Out out out of what?! what?! what?!"
said Woodpecker.

"Sticks," said the Icebear, pointing at
Castor the Beaver's dam. "And stones." He
pointed at Bear's cave.

Everyone gasped.

"That's Castor's house!" said Owl.

"And Bear's home!" said Vole.

Bear thought she had better fix this
terrible misunderstanding. "We will be
happy to help you find somewhere to live
in our Valley," she said. "But you can't just
take other people's homes."

"No, no, no." The Icebear shook his head.
"You don't understand. This is MY Valley
now, not yours."

Mole finally popped up out of the ground, leaving a big hole.

"Ah!" said the Icebear. "You've built the Royal Toilet just in time ..." And he pooped on Mole's head.

Mole gasped in shock. "I thought this kind of terrible thing only happened in books!" he said.

"If you don't want to be pooped on, don't sit in my toilet," said the king.

"But," gasped Vole, "if you take Bear's cave, and Castor's dam, and Mole's tunnel ... Where will WE all live?"

"Oh, somewhere else," said the king, waving a giant paw. "A nice desert maybe. Or a lovely swamp. Or a charming volcano."

"I don't WANT to live in a desert!" said Rabbit. "There's no GRASS in a desert!"

"I don't WANT to live in a swamp!" said Mole. "I can't tunnel in a swamp!"

"I don't WANT to live in a volcano," said Vole, and her voice trembled. "I don't even know what a volcano IS!"

"Ah, but what YOU want doesn't MATTER," said the king. "The only thing that matters is what *I* want."

"WHY?!" shouted all the animals.

"Because I am the King," said the Icebear. And he smiled, to show his enormous teeth, and – snick! – he slid out his enormous claws.

"Whu... whu... what ..." said Vole.

"Shut up! No more questions! You are making me THIRSTY with your questions. Bring me a drink."

"But everything is frozen," said Rabbit.

"THAT'S YOUR FAULT! Who has the biggest eyes? You!" The king picked up Owl, poked her in the tummy till she cried, and drank her tears.

"Hmmm. Not bad … Bit salty, though,"
said the king. "YOUR FAULT, STUPID
OWL!"

The animals were so shocked, they
couldn't speak.

Bear felt she had to do something.
"Don't you understand?"
she said. "We are
trying to *give* you our
friendship."

"I would rather *take* your *Valley*," said the Icebear King.

Bear was stunned. What else can I do? she thought. I must try EVERYTHING.

And so she tried to be even MORE friendly.

Then she tried to be helpful.

Then nice.

Then kind.

Nothing worked. Whatever she did, the king was horrible. Finally, as the sun went down and the moon came up, Bear said in despair, "But ... Can we *never* work together?"

"Just build me my Palace, slaves!" roared the king. "And if it isn't ready by dawn ... I will eat all of you!"

The animals gasped in horror.

"But build it quietly," said the king.
"Because I will be having a Royal Nap."
And he pulled a huge boulder over the
mouth of Bear's cave.

Soon he was snoring so loudly, snow fell
off the branches all around.

What a horrible day THAT was! thought
Rabbit, looking around at all his friends
sitting shivering in the moonlight. Then he
cheered up. "OK, Bear!" he said. "Save us!"
And he sat back happily.

There was a long pause.

TOO long …

Bear finally spoke, in a sad, quiet voice.
"I don't know how."

The animals couldn't believe their ears.

"But you always saved us from monsters before!" squeaked Vole.

"Why not *this* time?" said Rabbit.

"Being nice and friendly works with *most* animals," explained Bear. "Though it might take a while …" She glanced at Rabbit. Rabbit blushed. "But I cannot reach this king's heart. Something inside him is broken. He's become … nasty."

"Then … how do we fix this broken King of the Nasties?" said Rabbit.

"I don't think we can," said Bear. "He has to want to fix himself."

"But … he doesn't *want* to," said Rabbit.

"Maybe somebody pooped on his head as a cub," said Mole, "and he wants *us* to feel as bad *now* as he felt *then*."

"Oh dear. Now I feel sorry for him, and I don't *want* to feel sorry for him," said Rabbit.

"He is as nasty as … as … as … Wolf!" squeaked Vole.

"No," said Bear. "Wolf is mean because he is cold, and hungry, and has no friends. This king is mean because he enjoys it."

"Maybe we could … *scare* the king away? Some … hoo … hoo … how?" said Owl.

Bear shook her head. "An icebear is the scariest animal in the world. Stronger than a tiger, or a lion … or even me."

"But … he's scared of wolves, right?" said Rabbit. "EVERYBODY'S scared of wolves!"

"Yes," said Bear, "but it takes a LOT of wolves to scare just one icebear. And we don't have any wolves at all."

Bear looked the saddest they had ever seen her.

Oh no … thought Rabbit. It's all my fault we don't have Wolf around. *He* could have helped us find more wolves.

Rabbit opened his mouth, to ask Bear to go to the Dark Woods, and find Wolf, and say sorry, and ... But he closed his mouth again.

No, he thought. I can't ask Bear to fix all my mistakes. *I* must fix this.

And so Rabbit crept away, and walked in the moonlight towards the Dark Woods.

When he got to the edge of the woods, Rabbit trembled. The woods were vast. Where would he find Wolf?

He searched until he found the deepest, darkest place, where the shadows lived.

If I am going to find Wolf ... *that* is where, thought Rabbit.

But did he even WANT to find Wolf?

He took a deep breath ... another ... and walked straight into the darkness.

It was the longest, spookiest walk of Rabbit's life.

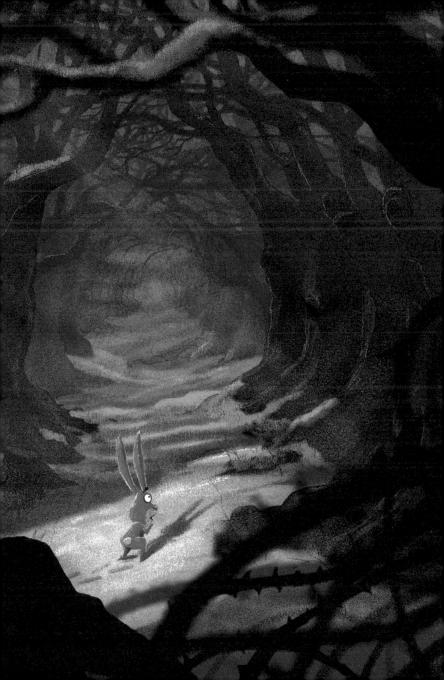

Finally, in the deep, dark heart of the woods, the ground began to rise. Rabbit saw he was climbing a white mountain, under a crisp white moon.

Rabbit turned and looked back. Far below, and all around him, stretched the Dark Woods.

"Wolf," he called softly. Rabbit secretly hoped Wolf wouldn't hear. But Wolf's hearing was VERY good.

Wolf loomed up between the dark roots of the highest tree on the mountain.

"Oh, *you*," said Wolf, and his teeth gleamed in the moonlight.

"Wolf," said Rabbit, his voice trembling. "I need your help."

"And I need my breakfast," said Wolf. "And my lunch. And my dinner ... But a midnight snack will do." He opened his jaws wide.

"Wait! Before you eat me ... There is something important you need to know."

Wolf paused. "More important than ... *food?*"

"Yes!" And Rabbit told Wolf the sad story of the bad king.

"How is this *my* problem, HMMMM?" growled Wolf. "*You* said I'm not even part of this Valley."

"I was wrong ... you *are* part of this Valley," said Rabbit. "We need you."

"Oh yeah?" sneered Wolf. "Why should I *care* if he eats all of you?"

"Because when he's finished with us," said Rabbit, "he'll eat you too."

"*Hmmm* ..." Wolf thought about this.

"Please," said Rabbit. "What should we do?"

Wolf shrugged. "Easy. Fight him, and defeat him."

"But my teeth can barely defeat *grass*," said Rabbit. "I once fought a dandelion, and it *won*."

"Good point," said Wolf, and he pulled some holly and ivy from the trunk of the old tree. "OK. Put on this crown."

KAPOW!

"Crown?" Rabbit was confused.

"That icebear is not your king," said Wolf. "No one is. You are the King of Yourself."

"Hurray!" said Rabbit, and stood taller. He felt more powerful already.

"And you need to carry this ..." Wolf handed Rabbit a curved branch from the tree.

"What is it?"

"It's a magic sword," said Wolf.

Rabbit hopped up and down with excitement. "*Really?*" he said.

"No," sighed Wolf, "it's just a stupid bendy stick. But I'm trying to trick you into being brave, so go along with me here and pretend it's magic."

Rabbit's ears drooped. "I don't think tricks work so well if you TELL the person it's a trick," he said.

"Really?" said Wolf. "Blast."

"Also, I don't know how to use a bendy stick," said Rabbit. "Er, I mean, a magic sword."

"I will show you," said Wolf. "First, we need to build a giant icebear ..." He shaped a snowdrift into an icebear. Then he snapped off some huge icicles from the tree. "These will make grrrrreat teeth!"

"Too scary!" Rabbit shuddered and turned away.

"Look at it!" ordered Wolf.

"WHY?!"

"Because if you are too scared even to *look* at a *fake* icebear, you will be far too scared to *fight* a *real* one."

Rabbit looked straight at it, his tummy trembling … But, to his surprise, the longer he looked, the more his fear shrank.

"I'm … not terrified any more!"

"Good," said Wolf, and Rabbit looked away, with a sigh of relief. "But not good enough!" roared Wolf. "I want you to look at this icebear until you are *bored*."

"Bored?"

"BORED!"

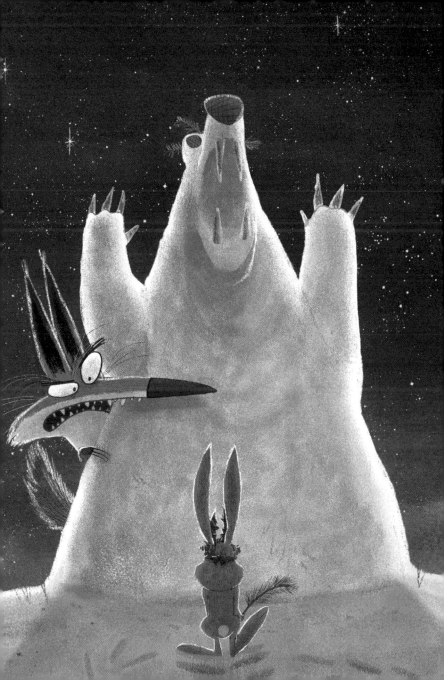

Rabbit looked. And looked. And the fear shrank and shrank, until eventually ... Rabbit yawned!

"How do you feel?" asked Wolf.

"OK," squeaked Rabbit. "I think."

"Good. Now, take a step ... towards it."

Rabbit gulped, and took a step towards the icebear, holding his bendy stick like a magic sword.

And his fear shrank even more.

"See?" said Wolf. "First defeat your fear. Then defeat your enemy."

Rabbit swung his magic bendy stick sword with a swish.

"Hey!" said Rabbit. "I *do* feel braver! ... Just a little bit," he added hastily. "But ..." Rabbit had an idea. "If I'm King of Myself, I order myself ... to be INFINITELY brave!"

He looked inside himself for infinite bravery.

Oh no! There was *some* new bravery; but there were also lots of little quivers of fear and shivers of worry, like always. "BAD RABBIT!!! YOU—"

"No!" Wolf raised a paw. "Rule yourself WISELY! You can't just order yourself to do *impossible* things."

"You are right, Wolf," said Rabbit. And he spoke more kindly to himself. "Do your best, Rabbit," he murmured. "*Try* to be brave. But I will understand if you are not."

"Good," said Wolf. "That's better. Now that you're a wise, kind King of Yourself, a wolf will run at your side, and help you."

"You, Wolf?"

"No; your own special wolf."

Rabbit sniffed the air, but he couldn't smell another wolf. "Where is he?"

"He will appear, as soon as you leave the woods."

Rabbit felt happier; but then he remembered how big and mean the Icebear was.

"Yes, but we will need ... one, two, three ..." Rabbit counted until he ran out of numbers, "... a HUGE number of wolves to defeat him!"

"You *have* a huge number of wolves," said Wolf.

"But *where are they?*" cried Rabbit in despair.

"Bring the other animals to the cliff at the edge of the woods," said Wolf.

By the time Rabbit got back, it was almost dawn. He saw Bear in the distance, and ran to give her a Bear-sized hug.

"Oooof," said Bear, hugging back. "I was *missing* you."

"I missed you, too," said Rabbit. "There was a Bear-shaped hole where you are meant to be."

"Rabbit! We thought the king had already EATEN you!" cried the animals. "Where did you *go?*"

Rabbit pointed. "I'll show you. Come with me."

"Come with you *into the Dark Woods?*" cried the animals.

"Just the edge!" said Rabbit. "It is better than being eaten at dawn."

The animals stared at the Dark Woods. Behind them, the rickety palace they had been trying to build collapsed for the fiftieth time.

They looked at the sad pile of sticks and stones, and listened as the king's angry snores grew louder.

They were tired and grumpy and desperate: and so they followed Rabbit to the Dark Woods.

Wolf explained the plan.

Vole gasped. "But we might be beaten!" She thought for a second. "And *eaten!*" She thought for another second. "And pooped!"

Wolf shrugged. "Yes," he said, "you might."

"Hey!" said Vole. "You are meant to say something to make me feel better!"

"Better? OK," said Wolf. "If you *don't* try this plan ... you will *definitely* be beaten, eaten, and pooped."

"That didn't help," said Vole, in a small voice.

Mole turned pale, which is a very difficult thing for a mole to do. "It's our only chance," he said. "We have to do it."

The animals nodded a yes that was so gloomy, it felt like a no.

Wolf gave each animal their own crown, and sword. And he taught them everything he had taught Rabbit.

As he taught them, they stood taller; and as they stood taller, the sun came up.

"Oh!" said Vole. "Now I get it! Bravery doesn't mean feeling no fear! It means feeling fear and *doing it anyway* ..."

"Yyyyeeeesss," said Wolf, "but—"

Vole charged towards the cliff's edge, shouting, "I'm not scared of you, scary cliff!"

"STOP!!!" Rabbit grabbed her tail, and dragged her back from the edge.

"As I was saying," said Wolf,
"sometimes fear is right, and you
must *listen*, and take a step *backwards*."

"Oh, that's complicated," sighed Vole.
"Growing up is hard."

"Yes," said Wolf. "It is. OK, let's go."

The animals took a deep breath.

Then, with their wonky crowns and their silly swords, they all took a step forward into the bright sunshine, on to the crisp snow.

And, as each animal took that first step, a black, silent wolf appeared at their side.

"Ooooh," gasped the animals, and all the wolves silently opened their mouths wide.

At last, they arrived at Bear's cave.

Rabbit said, "Icebear!" The snoring continued. He cleared his throat, and shouted, "ICEBEAR!"

The snoring stopped. The rock rolled aside. The Icebear stepped out.

"Icebear? ICEBEAR?!" he roared, rubbing the sleep out of his eyes. "CALL ME YOUR KING, OR I WILL EAT YOU!"

He walked towards Rabbit, without even bothering to look at him and his wolf, and kicked at the sad pile of sticks and stones.

"Where is my Palace?"

The animals had forgotten how big, and strong, and loud, and scary the real Icebear was.

Rabbit and his wolf took a step backwards. And another.

And so did all the other animals.

And so did all their wolves.

Until they reached the safety of the trees …

The other animals looked at Rabbit. What should they do now?

Rabbit felt like running away. No, he thought: I have a strong black wolf by my side. Rabbit glanced down … and saw that his dark silent wolf had vanished. Oh no, thought Rabbit. He looked around.

All their wolves had vanished.

The *cowards*, thought Rabbit fiercely.

"ANSWER ME!" roared the king, looking at Rabbit. "WHERE'S MY PALACE?"

Rabbit searched for a brilliant answer that would get him out of trouble. But all he could find was the Truth. Tell me, said the Truth, and see what happens.

"We are not building it," said Rabbit.

"NOT BUILDING IT!!!" roared the king.

"No," said Rabbit, in his firmest voice.

"Wait, what ... no?" said the Nasty Icebear King, in a much smaller voice. He was so big and scary that nobody had ever said no to him that firmly before.

"No!" squeaked Vole. Then she looked up at his enormous teeth, realised how brave she was being, and fainted. Bear picked her up.

"A bad king is a sad thing," said Rabbit, his voice quivering. "We will not help you any more."

The king growled so loudly, Rabbit
wobbled; but he kept looking the
Icebear straight in the eye, and held his
ground.

"You do not deserve to
be our king," said
Rabbit, growling a tiny
rabbit-growl.

You are an idiot, said Fear, popping up
in front of Rabbit. You just growled at the
biggest, baddest killer on earth.

Shut up, Fear, said Rabbit. I'm busy.

And Rabbit took a step forward, into the
heart of his fear; and through it, and out the
other side.

And now I am going to be eaten, thought
Rabbit. Oh well, at least I was brave ...

But the other animals wanted to
be brave like Rabbit, not scared like
themselves. They took a step forward,
too, and growled. And all the tiny growls
together sounded strangely like a roar.

And as they stepped forward into the
low winter sunlight, towards the thing they
feared ...

... all their wolves returned, and stood by their sides.

"WOLVES!" cried the king, taking a step backwards.

The animals and their wolves took
another step forward, and another, until
their noses were almost touching the king.
The whole valley seemed to freeze for a
silent second.

And then the Icebear seemed to shrink, and his shadow seemed to shrink …

"He's running away!! Backwards!" cried Rabbit, in astonishment and triumph.

The animals surged forward, and the Icebear ran away faster, and by the time the animals stopped at the edge of the lake, the king was a dot in the distance. And then he was gone.

"Hurray!!!" shouted Mole.

"Wow!" said Woodpecker. "Wow, Wow, Wow, Wow, Wow, Wow, Wow!!!"

Some of the animals were a little *too* excited by their new powers.

Mole got into a fight with a large bush,

Mouse attacked her own tail,

and Vole tried to eat
Bear. And their wolves
jumped all over the
place.

"What do we do about
all these *wolves*?"
said Owl nervously.

"You have won," said Wolf.
"Now you must lay down your swords, and
remove your crowns, or your wolves will
eat *you*."

The animals laid down their bendy magic swords, and their leafy crowns … and the wolves vanished.

Rabbit suddenly understood. "They were just our shadows all along!"

"Yes," said Wolf.

"Why didn't you *tell* us?" said Vole fiercely.

"The trick doesn't work as well if you TELL the person it's a trick," said Wolf.

"That's terrible!" said Vole. "We didn't have any help at all!"

Wolf smiled. "But that makes it even better! Those wolves were only your shadows; but your shadow is *part* of you. You defeated the bad king yourselves."

"We did? WE'RE WONDERFUL! Let's have a feast!" squeaked Vole.

"Mmm, yes, *let's*," said Wolf. His tummy rumbled enthusiastically.

The other animals all looked at him.

"What?" said Wolf, innocently.

"There is one *real* wolf left," said Owl. "One … real … hungry … Wolf."

"Maybe we should chase Wolf away, before he eats us for breakfast," whispered Vole.

But Rabbit shook his head, and said in a loud, clear voice, "Wolf is part of this Valley too. He worked with us to save it. We will all help to feed him."

Deep down, the animals knew this was fair. So they cheered, and ran home, and returned with food from their winter stores.

Together, they made Wolf some super-special sausages out of Bear's beetles' eggs, and Owl's dung beetles and Mole's worms and Woodpecker's grubs, seasoned with Rabbit's favourite herbs. There were so many sausages, they made Wolf a special sausage crown.

"Delicious," said Wolf, and his tummy gave a polite burp of agreement.

"Really?" said Rabbit.

"Well, as *food*," said Wolf, "... no."

"Oh dear," said Rabbit.

"But as a gift," said Wolf, "they DO taste of ... kindness."

"Well, we made them with thanks, and friendship, and love," said Rabbit.

"Yes, I could taste them," said Wolf. "The most delicious sauces in the world."

Rabbit looked around at all the animals. "We have changed ..." he said. "But have you, perhaps, changed too?"

"Hmm," said Wolf. "Now that I'm not starving ... and you have been so kind to me ... I suppose I don't feel *quite* as wolfish ..."

They looked at Wolf's shadow. It was shaped like a rabbit.

"Maybe we can be friends after all," said Wolf.

"I'd like that," said Rabbit.

Wolf pulled in his claws a little.

Rabbit pushed *out* his claws a little.

They smiled at each other, and shook hands.

"Let's play a board game," said Wolf.

"Yes!" said Rabbit and Bear and the other animals.

And they all played a giant board
game, with the frozen lake as the board.
It was the best game they'd ever played.

And Wolf didn't cheat once,
or eat *any* of his new friends.

LOOK OUT FOR MORE

RABBIT & BEAR

BOOKS COMING SOON!

FIND OUT WHAT HAPPENS NEXT IN:

This Lake is Fake!

Julian Gough

© Andreas Riemenschneider 2015

Julian Gough is an award-winning novelist, playwright, poet, musician and scriptwriter. He was born in London, grew up in Ireland and now lives in Berlin.

Among many other things, Julian wrote the ending to **Minecraft**, the world's most successful computer game for children of all ages.

He likes to drink coffee and steal pigs.

Jim Field is an award-winning illustrator, character designer and animation director. He grew up in Farnborough, worked in London and now lives in Paris.

His first picture book, **Cats Ahoy!**, written by Peter Bently, won the Booktrust's Roald Dahl Funny Prize. He is perhaps best known for drawing frogs on logs in the bestselling **Oi Frog!**

He likes playing the guitar and drinking coffee.

Jim Field

© Sandy Foucherand 2016